The Life and Adventures of
SANTA CLAUS

by L. Frank Baum
retold by Janeen R. Adil

·

Illustrated by Charles Santore

RP|KIDS
PHILADELPHIA · LONDON

PART ONE

A Baby Comes To Burzee

I N THE GREAT FOREST OF BURZEE, ANCIENT TREES GREW SO THICKLY THAT THEIR BRANCHES LACED TOGETHER, FORMING A LEAFY ROOF OVER-HEAD. HERE AND THERE A SUNBEAM SLIPPED THROUGH, LIGHTING up the mossy earth beneath. It was a place of deep shadows and even deeper quiet. Only the wild creatures broke the silence with their songs and cries.

Yet the Forest of Burzee was a home, too, although not to humans. For only the immortals, the Fairies, Knooks, Ryls, and Nymphs, lived here. In the depths of the forest these beings made their peaceful, happy homes.

The wood-nymph Necile was one of these who dwelt in Burzee. No one could say how old she was. Necile, however, looked as fresh and lovely as the day she was first cre-ated. Her job then had been to guard the forest and to protect the young trees. With her sister nymphs, Necile had helped the trees grow strong and sturdy.

But now Necile had little to occupy her days. There were, of course, times of pleas-ure. At each full moon came dancing, in the Royal Circle of the Queen Zurline. Special ceremonies, too, were held throughout the year. The Feast of Nuts, the Jubilee of Autumn Tintings, Leaf Shedding, and Budding Day were each celebrated by the forest-dwellers.

But Necile was restless. She longed for something to bring excitement and interest to her days. No other nymph, though, shared her thoughts. Only Necile was discontented with her life in the Forest of Burzee.

One evening, the great Ak came to visit the Forest. Ak, the Master Woodsman of the world, saw everything and knew more than any human. That night Queen Zurline sat beside him, while Necile and the other nymphs gathered at his feet. As the wise Ak spoke to them, Necile listened thoughtfully.

"Our life in this lovely forest," Ak began, "is one of joy and pleasure. How can we understand the sadness and misery that humans face? But it is good for us to show them compassion."

"I am sure, Ak," exclaimed the Queen, "that *you* have helped these poor humans!"

Ak smiled. "I have," he said. "More than once I have helped the very young ones that the humans call 'children.'"

"In fact," Ak went on, "tonight as I came to the edge of the Forest, I heard a weak cry. I looked around, and there, lying helpless in the grass, was a tiny baby! Then I called to the lioness Shiegra. I commanded her to give the baby milk and to keep it warm. I also told Shiegra to send word to every forest creature, saying that no one is to harm this child!"

The Queen was glad to hear this, and said so to Ak. Necile, however, slipped away from the group.

Running swiftly, Necile soon reached the edge of Burzee. Never before had she been so far from home. It was the Law of the Forest that nymphs live in the heart of the woods. And now she was breaking the Law.

Necile knew this. But there were no children among the immortals, only grown-ups. And so her desire to see a human child was stronger than this rule. As she looked through the trees, she spied the baby lying on the grass. Necile knelt beside it and stared in wonder.

"Necile's Little One"

SUDDENLY, AK STOOD UP. "I feel a strange presence in the Forest," he said.

At that, the Queen and the nymphs turned around. There before them was Necile, the sleeping baby in her arms, and a challenging look in her eyes.

For a moment, no one spoke but only stared in shock and surprise. At last, though, the Master Woodsman smiled, and kissed Necile on the forehead.

"Never before," he said, "has a nymph defied me and broken my Laws. I will not scold you but only ask: What do you want, Necile?"

Trembling a little, the nymph knelt before Ak. "Let me keep this child!"

"Here in Burzee, where no human has ever come?"

"Yes, here," Necile said to him. "I need a task, and this baby is helpless."

Ak frowned. "And what of the Law?"

"The Master Woodsman made the Law," replied the nymph. "He himself saved this child from death. So if he allows me to take care of it, who would dare to argue?"

Queen Zurline laughed. "You are trapped, Ak! Now, please consider Necile's request."

Deep in thought, Ak stroked his graying beard. At last he declared, "She shall keep the baby, and I will protect it. But I warn you! This is the first time that I have let my Law be broken, and it will be the last. Never again will an immortal adopt a human."

The meeting over, Ak left the Forest. Necile hurried to her cozy home beneath an oak tree, eager to settle in with her precious child.

Necile's snug little nest became the most popular place in Burzee. The nymphs gathered around to see the tiny baby, curious and delighted at the sight. They all praised Ak's kindness in allowing Necile to adopt this child.

Queen Zurline visited, too. Holding a chubby baby hand in hers, she spoke to Necile. "What shall we call him? He must have a name!"

"We will call him Claus," the nymph said, "since that means, 'a little one.'"

"We will call him Neclaus, instead," the queen decided, "meaning, 'Necile's little one.'"

This pleased all the nymphs, and so the baby became Neclaus. To Necile, however, he would always be Claus.

And so Necile set about making a good home for the child. She gathered soft moss for his bed, placing it beside her own. The animals helped, too. The gentle does and the lioness Shiegra gave milk to feed him.

Soon the other immortals came to visit, for the news about Claus spread quickly. They were curious to see this boy who had been adopted by the nymphs.

First to come were the Ryls, whose job was to watch over the flowers and plants. They were responsible for giving plants the dye that created the flowers' wonderful colors. The busy, cheerful Ryls were very popular with the other immortals.

Next to visit were the Knooks. Their task was to watch over all the tame and wild animals of the world. This difficult work made the Knooks rather old and tired-looking, and their manners were a little rough.

Finally the Fairies paid a visit, too. Their job was to act as invisible guardians to humankind. The Fairies' laws forbid the adoption of a human child, and so they were especially curious to see this little boy.

The baby Claus grew strong and healthy. Before long Necile was teaching him to walk and talk. He became a sweet and loving child, for like the nymphs, Claus was pure in heart. The little boy was free to wander wherever he liked. Because he was under Ak's protection, no creature would ever harm him.

Claus promptly made friends with all the immortals. The Ryls loved his laughter, the Knooks loved his courage, and the Fairies loved his innocence. In turn, Claus learned all their laws, protecting the flowers and respecting the beasts of the Forest.

Claus, however, knew nothing about the humans that the Fairies protected. The boy, who was quite happy in his forest home, believed he was the only one of his kind. Claus simply had no idea that millions of human beings lived and worked in the world outside the Forest of Burzee.

Claus Grows Up

THE YEARS FLEW BY, and Claus was soon a young man. Claus had learned the habits of every living creature in Burzee.

All this time Ak had had been visiting his other forests throughout the world. Finally, one day he returned to the great Forest of Burzee. Queen Zurline and her nymphs gathered to greet him. As the nymphs sat in a circle before the Master Woodsman, Claus took his place among them.

Ak was unusually quiet. He had looked deep into Claus's eyes and was pleased to find him a brave and innocent youth. Nevertheless, Ak spent a good deal of time stroking his beard, deep in thought.

By the next morning, Ak had made a decision. "Tell Necile and the other nymphs good-bye," he said to Claus. "You shall come with me on my journey around the world."

Claus was very happy at the thought of accompanying the Master Woodsman. But Necile cried for the first time in her long life. Although she knew Claus would return, she loved him deeply. It was hard to see him go.

As they prepared to leave, Ak gave the young man instructions. "You must hold tightly onto my sash," he said. "Do this, and you will be invisible. If you let go, however, you can never return to your home in Burzee!"

Claus did as he was told and held on tightly. And then they were off, flying through the air, very high and very fast.

When tall buildings appeared below them, Ak brought them down into the center of the city. Claus stared in wonder. After life among the immortals, he had thought that there was no one like him in the world. Yet here were humans everywhere!

The astonished young man looked carefully at the faces around him. Happy, sad, rich, poor, proud, humble—there were all sorts of people. But what interested Claus the most were the children. He loved to watch them, although what he saw puzzled him.

"Why," Claus asked, "aren't all these little ones alike? Some play with sticks, and others play with golden toys."

"Some were born into poor families," Ak replied. "Others were born into rich ones. All babies, however, are sweet and innocent. They are happy simply to be alive. It's when these little ones grow up that they change. Then work and worry about making money weigh them down."

After a moment's silence, Claus said, "Why was I born in the Forest?"

Ak told him the story of how he had been found as a baby. "You were raised by immortals, who will live forever. You are human, and must grow old," he added gently. "But wise humans look for ways to help the world. In this way their good deeds live forever."

When at last they returned to Burzee, Queen Zurline and her nymphs gathered to welcome the travelers home. Then, at a word from Ak, Claus stood up and addressed the group.

"I never knew who or what I was, until the great and kind Ak showed me. Now I know I am a human. Like all people, I must make my way upon the earth and then leave it behind. And like all people, my job is to make the world a little better."

Claus turned to Necile. "I will love you forever. But now I must leave and begin to live my life as a human."

"What will you do?" asked the queen.

"I will dedicate myself to children and try to make them happy. I will do this to honor Necile, and all of you, who took such loving care of me when I was a tiny baby."

Now Ak stood up. "You have spoken well. And now I tell you that even though you will go into the world of humans, you will still be protected. You may always call upon the Nymphs, the Ryls, the Knooks, and the Fairies for help. I, the Master Woodsman of the World, say this. It is my Law!"

PART TWO

The Laughing Valley

PAST THE EASTERN EDGE OF BURZEE LAY THE LAUGHING VALLEY OF HOHAHO. SUN SHONE ON GENTLE GREEN HILLS AND SPARKLED OFF A RUSHING BROOK. BEES BUZZED OVER THE WILD-FLOWERS DOTTING the grass. A breeze caught Claus's hair, and he exclaimed with joy, "Here is where I will make my home!"

Claus knew that like other humans, he would need a house. He was unsure of how to begin, until suddenly old Nelko appeared at his side. Nelko, who was Ak's servant, carried a sturdy ax with a silvery blade. Without a word, he handed the ax to Claus and then disappeared.

Now Claus understood what to do. To cut down a living tree was unthinkable—the nymphs had taught him that. But there were plenty of fallen trees at the Forest's edge. Claus set to work cutting and trimming these into logs. By nightfall, he had prepared enough logs to build a home. The young man stretched out on the grass and fell into a deep and peaceful sleep.

As Claus slept, the Knooks came to the Laughing Valley. Quickly and quietly they fitted the logs together into a strong and roomy house. When Claus awoke the next morning and discovered their gift, his heart was filled with gratitude to his friends.

Claus spent a happy day listening to the songs of brook, flowers, and sun. He chatted with ants and beetles, and joked with butterflies. That night, when he lay down to sleep, he was perfectly contented.

Once again, as Claus slept, visitors came to the Valley. This time it was the Fairies, who brought with them dishes and pans for the home, and clothing for Claus. And once again, Claus was grateful to his thoughtful friends.

Making Toys

CLAUS HAD CHOSEN to become a friend to children, and right away he began to search them out. He walked to the plain beyond the Valley, and beyond the plain, too, looking for homes where children lived. Soon every baby and child knew his loving face and joyful smile.

Claus quickly made friends with them all. They played games with him, and rested comfortably in his strong arms. Claus could make a sick child feel better, or a sad child, cheerful. Wherever he went, happiness and laughter followed.

There were only two homes where Claus was not welcome. One was the palace of the Lord of Lerd. The other was the castle of the Baron Braun. Children lived at both places, but when Claus tried to see them, he was rudely turned away.

When winter came, deep snow covered the Laughing Valley. In his log home, Claus sat warm and snug by the fire. Sitting with him was Blinkie, a large, glossy black cat given him by Peter the Knook.

"This snow will keep me from playing with the children," Claus told the cat. "It will be a long time before I see them again."

Since the immortals were providing his food and firewood, there was little for Claus to do. He soon became restless. One evening, he picked up a stick and started carving it with his sharp knife. As he worked, Claus whistled and sang while Blinkie purred contentedly.

Suddenly, Claus stopped working and stared in surprise at the piece of wood. Without realizing it, he had begun to carve the head of a cat! This gave him an idea. Using Blinkie as a model, Claus spent the rest of the evening carving. When he was done, he had created a life-like wooden cat. Claus had just made his first toy.

Claus gave away this toy cat to a small boy. It was hard to tell who was most delighted: the child with his gift, or the kind-hearted young man. And so Claus set to work and carved another wooden cat. Then he thought of carving other animals, ones that young children might like. Deer, rabbits, lambs, and squirrels, he decided, would be gentle animals that children would love.

Claus was helped in his work by his friends, the immortals. The Red Ryl, the Black Ryl, the Green Ryl, the Blue Ryl, and the Yellow Ryl all brought him their paints to use. These were colors that the Ryls used to paint the wildflowers. They also brought Claus brushes, made from the tips of a sturdy grass.

The Knooks supplied him with clear, soft wood that was good for carving. And the Fairies provided Claus with tools: knives, hammers, saw, chisels, and nails.

Claus turned his largest room into a workshop where he could spread out his tools and paints. All day long he worked on his toys. And all day long, he sang and laughed and whistled happily.

Rich and Poor

ONE DAY CLAUS HAD an unusual visitor. A young girl came riding up to his door, seated on a pure white horse. With her rode a score of knights in bright armor, sent to protect the child.

The visitor was Bessie Blithesome. She was the daughter of the Lord of Lerd, who had once sent Claus away from his palace. Now Bessie came to Claus with a request.

"Please," she said, "I want a toy! Yours are the most wonderful toys in the world."

Claus was quite surprised by this. "You are the daughter of a rich lord and can have anything you want," he said. "My toys are for poor children, who don't have the things you do."

"But don't both poor children and rich ones love to play with toys?" Bessie asked.

"I suppose so," said Claus, thoughtfully.

"Then why can't I have the toys I want? It's not my fault that other children are poorer than I am."

Bessie started to cry. "I will be so unhappy if I can't have the toys I want!"

Now Claus was troubled. His one desire was to make all children happy, whether they were rich or poor. Yet how could he give Bessie a toy when so many poor children were anxious to have one, too?

Claus made a decision. "The toys I am making now are promised to other children," he told the girl. "But since you want one so badly, you may have the next one I make. Come back in two days and it will be ready."

Delighted, Bessie gave Claus a kiss. Then, calling to her knights, the little girl rode away.

At the brook, Claus stopped for a drink. For a while he lay on the bank, playing with a piece of soft clay from the water's edge. Without thinking, he began modeling the earthy material with his fingers. All of a sudden, Claus realized that he had shaped the clay into a head—and the head looked a bit like Necile!

Claus had an idea. He dug up some more clay and brought it back to his workshop. There he modeled it, creating a body, arms, and legs to add to the head. Claus found, however, that because the clay was so soft, he had to work very gently so as not to ruin the figure. This led to another idea.

"I will lay this toy nymph in the sun," he decided. "The sun's rays may help the clay dry out and harden."

By the next morning, the clay was in fact hard as stone. Claus was quite pleased, and he set to work painting this new toy. With Necile as his inspiration, he painted deep blue eyes and rosy lips. Her gown was oak-leaf green and on her feet were sandals. When he was done, Claus thought his clay nymph was quite pretty.

The following day Bessie again rode up to his door. Claus handed her the new toy, and Bessie held it lovingly.

"What is it called?" she asked.

Claus thought for a moment. Then he said the first word that came to mind. "It's called a dolly," he told her.

"I love my dolly!" Bessie exclaimed, giving it a kiss. "Thank you, Claus!" And the child rode away, perfectly happy.

Seeing her joy, Claus began to create another doll. Once more he used soft clay from the brook to model a figure. But now he covered the clay figure with hot coals from the fireplace. Instead of waiting for the sun to dry the clay, the coals did the job quickly. Soon the clay doll was hard and dry.

The gown on Bessie's dolly had been made of clay. This time, however, Claus decided to use fabric. He called to the Fairies for help. They brought him a supply of colored silks, lace, and golden threads. "A child is sure to love this beautiful toy," he thought.

PART THREE

Delivering Toys

Now Claus was even busier than usual. Not only was he making toy animals, but also dolls in every size. Soon he began creating musical instruments, too, drums and whistles and horns.

Whenever Claus had a large supply of toys, he would load them into a huge sack. Then, swinging the sack over his shoulder, he would walk from village to village. Children everywhere were delighted to receive Claus's wonderful toys.

But when winter came again, Claus could no longer travel. Snow many feet deep covered the Laughing Valley. When Claus tried to walk through it, he sank up to his armpits.

One morning Claus looked out of his window and saw two deer nearby. They were Flossie and Glossie. Claus had known these deer in the Forest. When he called out to them, the deer stopped to talk.

Claus was surprised to see that they were walking on *top* of the snow.

"The Frost King breathed on it," explained Glossie. "The surface of the snow is as hard as ice!"

"If I could run like you," Claus said, "I could deliver all my toys. Or perhaps you could carry me on your back."

"No," replied Flossie, "you can't run like a deer. Nor can we carry you, since our backs aren't strong enough. But if you had a sleigh, you could harness us to it. Then we could easily pull you and your sack of toys as well."

Claus was delighted with this suggestion.

Claus went to work building a sleigh. From two long pieces of wood, he fashioned runners with up-turned ends at the front. Across these he nailed wooden boards to make a platform. Next he twisted and knotted strong cords together, creating a collar. With more cords he attached the collar to the front of the sleigh.

Glossie and Flossie returned before Claus had finished. Will Knook had given them permission to make this trip with Claus. The deer, however, had to be back in Burzee by dawn.

Claus hitched the two deer to the sleigh. Cords tied to their antlers would serve as reins. He added a small stool to sit on and placed a sack of toys at his feet.

"Away we go!" Claus shouted, and the deer sprang forward. Claus, the toys, the sleigh, and the deer sped over the ice-covered snow.

The travelers reached a small town, where Claus had never been before. Right away he saw a problem. Because it was nighttime, all the townspeople had gone to bed.

"The doors are locked," he said. "I can't get in, so I can't give the children their toys!"

Glossie, however, had a suggestion. "Why don't you climb down the chimney?" And with one leap, the deer had pulled the sleigh to the roof.

Claus was quite pleased with this plan. Slinging his sack of toys over his shoulder, he crept down the chimney. Inside the home, he lovingly placed toys next to the sleeping children in their beds. Then, his delivery completed, Claus climbed back up the chimney.

Flossie and Glossie leaped to the next roof. Before long, Claus had been down every chimney in the town. Each child would wake up the next morning to find a wonderful toy, given by the generous Claus.

From there they dashed to another village, and then on to a large city. At last the sack of toys was empty. Claus turned the deer towards home.

But in the east, the sky was growing lighter. It was nearly dawn! Now the deer flew over the snow, racing to be back in Burzee. Claus held on tightly until the sleigh came to a sudden stop. Claus tumbled out into the snow, right outside his own front door.

"Quickly," cried the deer, "cut away our harness!" Then, as dawn was breaking, Claus watched as the pair disappeared into the Forest.

Santa Claus

THAT MORNING WILL KNOOK came to see Claus. He was chief guardian of the deer and in a sour mood.

"Glossie and Flossie were one minute late," he complained, "and that is as bad as one hour. They must be punished for their disobedience."

"Please don't do that!" Claus begged. But Will Knook refused to listen and went away, grumbling.

With that, Claus set off into the Forest. Necile, he thought, could advise him on how to rescue the deer from their punishment. Claus was delighted to find not only Queen Zurline and her nymphs gathered together, but also his old friend, Ak.

After the Master Woodsman had heard Claus's story, he sent for the Prince of the Knooks, the Queen of the Fairies, and the Prince of the Ryls. Once again Claus told the story of his snowy journey by sleigh with the two deer.

Now Ak spoke to the Prince of the Knooks. "The good work that Claus is doing among the humans should be supported by the immortals. Already some are calling him a Saint. Soon people everywhere will know the name, Santa Claus!"

Ak went on. "Don't you agree that Claus deserves our friendship and encouragement? These deer are willing to pull his sleigh. I would beg you, then, to let Claus use their help!"

The other immortals agreed with the Master Woodsman. To the Knook Prince they offered services. They would protect the deer, as well as provide certain healthy plants for them to eat. They would also allow them to bathe in special waters, which would make their coats beautiful.

After more discussion, the Prince of the Knooks finally made a decision. "Once every year, on Christmas Eve, I will allow the deer to go with Claus. They must, however, return to the Forest by daybreak. He may choose up to ten deer to pull his sleigh. These we will call Reindeer, to tell them apart from the others. Now, my words shall be obeyed!"

And so that Christmas Eve found Claus once again ready to travel. Glossie and Flossie were harnessed to the sleigh. A sack brim-full of toys was at his feet. Again the moon rose over the sleepy, snowy land.

This time they set off in a new direction, to stop at homes where Claus had not yet visited. At each farmhouse and in every village, Claus crept down the chimneys. It gave him great joy to leave toys for all the little ones to find the next morning.

The two deer dashed from home to home as Claus laughed and sang. Then, when the sack of toys was finally empty, they headed home. The deer flew over the frozen ground and this time were back in Burzee before the break of dawn.

Claus, exhausted from the night's journey, fell into a deep sleep. It was his first Christmas Eve toy delivery, the first of many, many more to come!

Some New Customs

THE BARGAIN WITH the Knook Prince changed Claus's plans forever. By the Prince's order, the reindeer could pull the sleigh on only one night each year. The rest of the year, then, Claus would devote to making toys and so deliver them on Christmas Eve.

Claus realized that a year's worth of work would produce a huge number of toys. To carry them all he would need a new sleigh, a sleigh much larger and stronger than his old one.

His first step was to visit the Gnome King. In return for toys for his own children, the Gnome King gave Claus a pair of finely built steel runners. Another exchange of toys brought Claus two strings of jingling sleigh bells for the deer. Glossie and Flossie, he knew, would be delighted with the bells' sweet, ringing tones.

Next Claus chose thin, strong boards to construct his sleigh. For the front he built a high, curved dash-board, to keep off the snow flung from the reindeer's hooves. The sides were built high as well, to hold a quantity of toys. Claus then mounted the sleigh on the fine steel runners. Lastly he painted his sleigh in bright colors.

Flossie and Glossie came to look over Claus's work. They admired the big, handsome sleigh. It was, however, too large and heavy for them to pull.

Flossie made a suggestion. "The Prince of the Knooks allowed you up to ten deer to pull your sleigh. With a team of ten, we could travel like lightning!"

Claus thought this was an excellent idea. "Please go to the Forest at once," he told them. "Find eight other deer who are as similar to yourselves as possible. And be sure that you all eat the immortals' healthy plants and bathe in the special waters. Then by next Christmas Eve my reindeer will be the most beautiful and powerful in the world!"

Another Christmas Eve had arrived. At twilight, ten deer appeared at Claus's door. With Glossie and Flossie were Racer and Pacer, Reckless and Speckless, Fearless and Peerless, and Ready and Steady. Each reindeer had spreading antlers, dark velvety eyes, and a smooth brown coat. Claus had made a new harness of strong, soft leather. With it he hitched the reindeer by pairs to the sleigh. Flossie and Glossie, who were in the lead, wore the strings of sleigh bells. The two were so pleased with the bells' music that they pranced about, just to make them ring.

Claus seated himself in the sleigh. Over his knees he wrapped a warm blanket and pulled a fur hat over his ears. With him were three huge bags over-flowing with toys. Each corner of the sleigh was packed with gifts as well.

And then they were off! The ten reindeer leaped forward, swift as a wind. Claus laughed and sang as they began their yearly journey, delivering toys and spreading happiness to children.

It was on the following Christmas Eve that a new custom began. Four little children, who had been playing in the snow, came indoors with their socks soaked through and through. These wet stockings were hung up over the fireplace to dry.

The stockings were the first things Claus saw when he came down the chimney. As always, he was in a great hurry to deliver as many toys as possible. So he quickly stuffed toys into the socks and then dashed up the chimney again. To the reindeer's great surprise, Claus was back on the roof in a flash and ready to speed onward to their next stop.

"I wish all the children would hang up their stockings!" thought Claus. "It would save me a lot of time. Then I could visit even more children before dawn!"

The next morning, these children were delighted to find gifts from Santa Claus in their stockings. They told their friends all about it, and from there the word spread. Soon more and more children were hanging up their socks for Santa Claus to fill.

On his next visit, Claus discovered a great many stockings had been hung. He could fill these in a jiffy, which saved him time to make more visits. The custom grew each year, and it was a true help to Claus.

One year, just before their annual journey, a Fairy came to Claus. The Fairy told him of three small children who were terribly poor. They lived in a tent on a broad, treeless plain. Claus decided to make it a special point to visit them.

During his travels that night, Claus picked up the top of a pine tree, which the wind had broken off. When he reached the tent, he planted the bushy top in the sand. On the branches he hung candles, beautiful toys, and bags of candy.

"Merry Christmas, little ones!" Claus shouted into the tent. Then he leaped into his sleigh and was gone before they could see him.

This sparkling, marvelous tree filled the three children with wonder and joy. Claus was pleased, too, and so the next year he brought more trees with him. These he set up and decorated in the homes of other poor children.

In some houses, the parents were able to get their own trees. Then Santa Claus had only to add his gifts to the branches. As more and more people set up Christmas trees, another new custom was created.

Children looked forward eagerly to his visit each year. Everywhere he went, Santa Claus was welcomed with more excitement than the visit of any royal king.

PART FOUR

Old Claus Becomes Young Again

FOR A GREAT MANY YEARS CLAUS CARRIED ON HIS SPECIAL WORK. ALL YEAR LONG HE MADE THE MOST MARVELOUS TOYS. EACH CHRISTMAS EVE HE AND HIS REINDEER VISITED CHILDREN'S HOMES AROUND the world. And Claus was always strong, healthy, and happy as he brought joy to children everywhere.

But at last Claus grew old. His long beard, which had been golden brown, turned to gray, and then finally to pure white. His hair, too, grew white. Around his merry, laughing eyes, wrinkles creased his skin.

Then came a time when Claus could no longer make toys. His strength gone, he lay on his bed as if in a dream. Claus was slipping away from this world into the next.

The Nymph Necile, who had cared for and loved her Claus since he was a baby, was greatly troubled. She found Ak and informed him that their friend was dying. At this news, the Master Woodsman became very serious. He thought deeply for several minutes. Then a thought came to Ak, one that filled him with a powerful sense of purpose.

Immediately Ak sent messengers to all parts of the world. "Tonight," he told Necile, "the immortals will hold a council here in Burzee. If my advice is taken, Claus will drive his reindeer for ages yet to come!"

At midnight, the rulers of the immortals assembled in that ancient Forest. It was the first time in many centuries that they had come together like this. Their meeting was a strange and wondrous sight!

Among those gathered was the Queen of the Water Sprites, lovely as pure crystal. Next to her was the King of the Sleep Fays, who brought sleep to humans. The Gnome King was next, guardian of jewels and precious metals. Beside him was the King of the Sound Imps, responsible for carrying every sound that is made.

The King of the Wind Demons was present, too, along with the Fairy Queen and the King of the Light Elves. With them were the King of the Knooks and the King of the Ryls. Rounding out the circle was Queen Zurline of the Wood-Nymphs.

Two other immortals sat in the center of the circle with Ak, the Master Woodsman. With him was Kern, the Master Husbandman of the World. Kern ruled the grain fields, the meadows, and the gardens. The third was Bo, Master Mariner of the World, ruler of the seas and ships. These three were so important that all of the other immortal Kings and Queens bowed down to them.

"What do you wish, Ak?" called out the King of the Wind Demons.

Ak spoke up boldly. "To give Claus the Cloak of Immortality!"

At once there were exclamations of surprise. The immortals questioned Ak, pointing out that no human had ever been granted this before.

"I know this," replied Ak. "But the Supreme Master created the Cloak of Immortality for a purpose. Who else besides Claus deserves it? The Cloak isn't of any use unless it's worn. Won't you all vote to give it to this man, Claus?"

Then one after another the Queens, Kings, Kern, and Bo cast their votes. And so it was granted that Claus would receive immortality!

Then the immortals carried the Cloak to the Laughing Valley. They gathered around Claus's bed and softly laid the garment over him. The Cloak wrapped itself around Claus and sank, disappearing into his body. It had become part of him and could never be taken away. The immortals departed, glad to have given the precious Cloak to this good man.

When Claus awoke the next morning, he was astonished to find himself feeling strong and healthy once again. He jumped from his bed and stood at the window, the bright sun pouring in on him. Claus had no idea what had happened to him. But although his beard was still snowy white, he had the energy of a young man. Now Claus again busied himself making new toys, whistling happily all the while.

Then Ak came to see him. He told Claus how he had been given the Cloak of Immortality, and why. Claus grew very serious as he heard the story, aware of the honor that had been done to him.

And so for generation after generation, Santa Claus continued his generous work. All year he created wonderful toys, delivering them to delighted children everywhere on Christmas Eve. These little ones loved him dearly. The parents honored him for the joy he brought. The grandparents were grateful to him, remembering their own youthful happiness.

Was it ever too much work for the beloved old fellow?

Claus's reply came with a merry laugh. "In all this world there is nothing so beautiful as a happy child," he said. "As long as there are children in the world I will strive to make them happy."

To Nellie and Charlie Hart
and our life on Fulton Street

Illustrations © 2009 by Charles Santore

All Rights reserved under the Pan-American and
International Copyright Conventions

Printed in China

9   8   7   6   5   4   3   2   1

Digit on the right indicates the number of this printing.

Library of Congress Control Number: 2009922632

ISBN 978-0-7624-2796-3

Cover and interior design by Frances J. Soo Ping Chow
Edited by Kelli Chipponeri
Typography: Adobe Caslon, Snell Roundhand, and Trajan

Published by Running Press Kids, an imprint of
Running Press Book Publishers
2300 Chestnut Street
Philadelphia, PA 19103-4371

Visit us on the web!
www.runningpress.com